There Is a Bird on Your Head!

To Lee and Diane

ISBN-13: 978-0-545-11598-8
ISBN-10: 0-545-11598-1

 Published by Scholastic Inc., 557 Broadway, New York, NY 10012, by arrangement with Hyperion Books for Children, an imprint of Disney Children's Book Group, LLC. SCHOLASTIC and associated logos are trademarks and/or registered trademarks of Scholastic Inc.

12 11 10 9 8 7 6 5 4 3 2 1 9 10 11 12 13/0

Printed in the U.S.A. 23

First Scholastic printing, January 2009

There Is a Bird on Your Head!

Mo Willems

An ELEPHANT & PIGGIE Book

SCHOLASTIC INC.
New York Toronto London Auckland Sydney
Mexico City New Delhi Hong Kong Buenos Aires

Piggie!

Is something on my head?

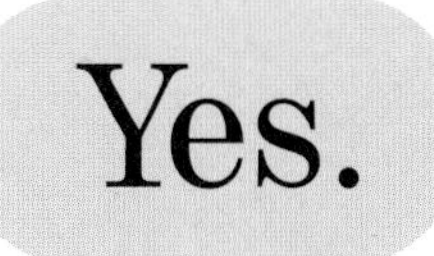
Yes.

There is a bird
on your head.

There is a bird
on my head?

Aaaaaaaa

ggghhh!!!

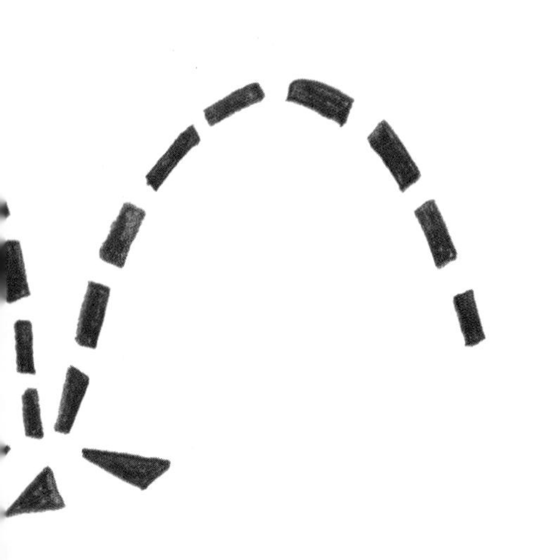

Is there a
bird on my
head now?

No.

Now there are two birds on your head.

What are two birds doing on my head?

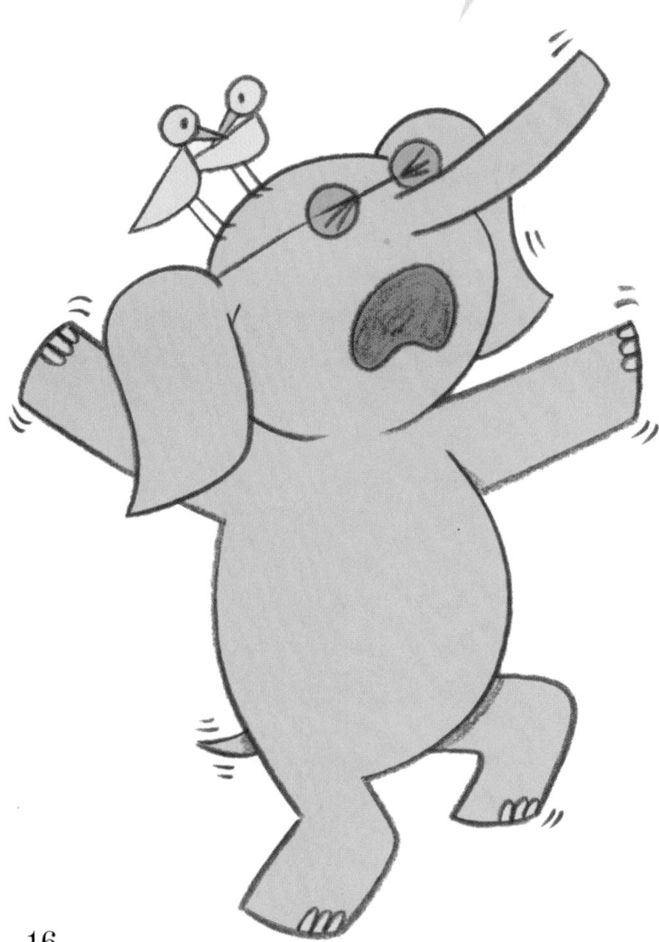

They are
in love!

The birds on my head are in love?

They are
love birds!

Love birds!

How do you
know they are
love birds?

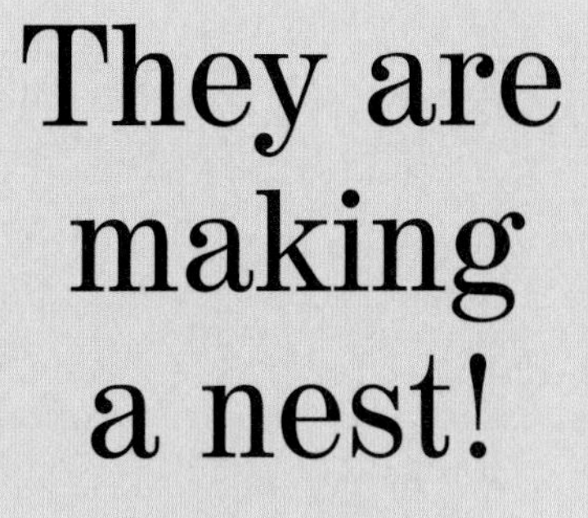
They are making a nest!

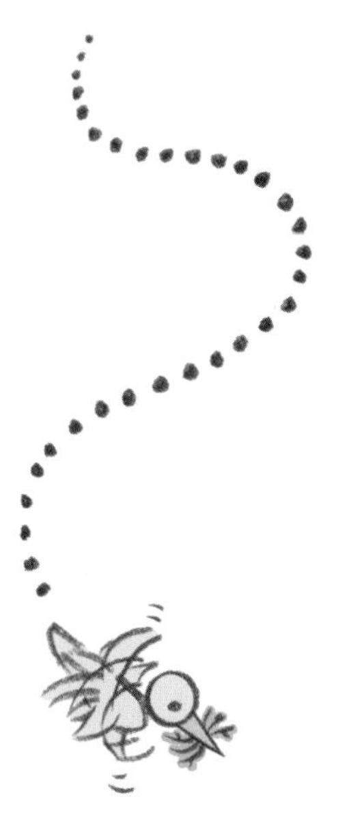

Two birds are making a nest on my head?

Why would two birds make a nest on my head?

I am afraid to ask . . .

Do I have an egg on my head?

One.

Two.

Three!

You have three eggs
on your head.

I do not want three eggs on my head!

Then I have good news!

The eggs are gone?

The eggs are hatching!

HATCHING?

The eggs on my head
are hatching?

Cheep!
Cheep!
Cheep!

They have hatched.

Now, I have three baby chicks on my head!

And two birds
and a nest!

I do not want three baby chicks, two birds, and a nest on my head!

Where do you want them?

SOMEWHERE ELSE!

Why not ask them to
go somewhere else?

Ask them?

Ask them!

Okay.
I will try asking.

Excuse me, birds.
Will you please go
somewhere else?

No
problem.

Bye!
It worked!

Now there are no
birds on my head!

Thank you, Piggie!
Thank you very much!

You are welcome. . . .